Constance Clarke is the global author of The Clarke Fables Collection. She was born in Dover-Foxcroft, Maine and was raised and lives in Schenectady, New York. Influenced by her grandfather, she enjoys writing poetry. As a retired teacher and grandmother of five, she has long understood that children learn so much through what they read, which is why she has combined her poetry with original fables. She volunteers with a school reading program, a regional rehabilitation hospital, and the theatre. She and her family enjoy their summers in the Adirondack Mountains.

Clarke Fables include: *The Monkey and the Tiger, The Elephant and the Jungle Bug, The Sun and the Moon, The Puffin and His Feathers, The Possum and the Owl, and The Toad and His Warts.*

CONSTANCE CLARKE

A Clarke Fable

THE PUFFIN
AND HIS Feathers

AUSTIN MACAULEY PUBLISHERS™

LONDON • CAMBRIDGE • NEW YORK • SHARJAH

Ordering Information

Quantity sales: Special discounts are available on quantity purchases by corporations, associations, and others. For details, contact the publisher at the address below.

Publisher's Cataloging-in-Publication data

Clarke, Constance
The Puffin and his Feathers

ISBN 9781638290285 (Paperback)
ISBN 9781638290445 (ePub e-book)

Library of Congress Control Number: 2023901859

www.austinmacauley.com/us

First Published 2023
Austin Macauley Publishers LLC
40 Wall Street, 33rd Floor, Suite 3302
New York, NY 10005
USA

mail-usa@austinmacauley.com
+1 (646) 5125767

iv

To every child who has experienced being sick.

Heartfelt thanks to the wonderful collaboration effort of my Austin Macauley Publisher Team!

The cottage window was wide open,
Breezy curtains floated through.
On the sill sat a little puffin,
Preening feathers, as birds do.

Puffin peered around the quiet room,
And he stretched in the sunlight.
On the wall there hung a framed mirror,
Which he gazed at with delight.

Several days passed before he returned,
The window was still open.
Gazing at his handsome self once more,
He stared. Then stood there frozen.

Feathers covering his head and neck,
Had all but disappeared.
His bill had shed all its colored plates!
All was lost, or so he feared.

Even his eyes, that had once been bright,
Had dark circles all around.
Sadly, he turned and hopped from the sill,
Landing softly on the ground.

More time went by. Wing feathers were lost,
As were some plumes from his tail.
What little he could see remaining,
Were no longer bright, but pale.

He'd always had trouble with landing,
Now he was a flightless bird!
Nor could he swim by flapping his wings!
But Puff would not be deterred!

He tried to keep his humor intact,
But thought this quite revolting.
Puff didn't understand what happened!
What was this thing called 'molting'?

All that night Puffin slept on the sill,
Awakened by morning sun.
An amazing surprise awaited!
Feathers had grown! One by one!

22

New feathers had pushed out the old ones,
And everything was brand new.
His bill was now better than ever!
He knew what he had to do!

Puff spread his wings and began to fly,
Over mountains and beyond.
New adventures were awaiting him!
A wonderful day had dawned!

Moral:
Going through troubling times can make
us stronger.

The cottage window was wide open
Breezy curtains floated through.
On the sill sat a little puffin,
Preening feathers, as birds do.

Puffin peered around the quiet room,
And he stretched in the sunlight.
On the wall there hung a framed mirror,
Which he gazed at with delight.

Several days passed before he returned,
The window was still open.
Gazing at his handsome self once more,
He stared. Then stood there frozen.

Feathers covering his head and neck,
Had all but disappeared.
His bill had shed all its colored plates!
All was lost, or so he feared.

Even his eyes, that had once been bright,
Had dark circles all around.
Sadly, he turned and hopped from the sill,
Landing softly on the ground.

More time went by. Wing feathers were lost,
As were some plumes from his tail.
What little he could see remaining,
Were no longer bright, but pale.

He'd always had trouble with landing,
Now he was a flightless bird!
Nor could he swim by flapping his wings!
But Puff would not be deterred!

He tried to keep his humor intact,
But thought this quite revolting…
Puff didn't understand what happened!
What was this thing called 'molting'?

All that night Puffin slept on the sill,
Awakened by morning sun.
An amazing surprise awaited!
Feathers had grown! One by one!

New feathers had pushed out the old ones,
And everything was brand new.
His bill was now better than ever!
He knew what he had to do!

Puff spread his wings and began to fly,
Over mountains and beyond.
New adventures were awaiting him,
A wonderful day had dawned!

30

Moral: Going through troubling times can make us stronger.

CPSIA information can be obtained
at www.ICGtesting.com
Printed in the USA
JSHW072233110623
43035JS00003B/8

9 781638 290285